Enjoy!!

Papi and the Miracle

A Little Donkey Adventure

Sherri Weston Martel

WestBow Press books may be ordered through booksellers or by contacting:

WestBow Press
A Division of Thomas Nelson & Zondervan
1663 Liberty Drive
Bloomington, IN 47403
www.westbowpress.com
1 (866) 928-1240

ISBN: 978-1-5127-6163-4 (sc)
ISBN: 978-1-5127-6162-7 (e)

Library of Congress Control Number: 2016917801

Print information available on the last page.

WestBow Press rev. date: 10/26/2016

WESTBOW
P R E S S®
A DIVISION OF THOMAS NELSON
& ZONDERVAN

Papi and the Miracle

A Little Donkey Adventure

Based on Zechariah 9:9 & Matthew 21:6-8

Of the Holy Bible

Papi was born on a warm spring day long ago. The first thing he saw was the green green grass, all shiny with dew. The first thing he heard was the voice of his mother Nika, who gently whispered "Wake up little one!"

And Papi began his first day.

The hill where Papi first stood on his wobbly legs was high and wide and stretched down, down into the valley below.
"Does it all belong to us?" asked Papi.

"Yes." said Nika proudly.

Soon Papi's legs were strong and straight. He could run and jump without falling. In the wide meadow he saw other donkeys like himself, with long grey ears and big brown eyes.

"Who are they?" he whispered to Nika.

His mother smiled. "Those are your cousins, Papi."

"Oh!" said Papi.

2

The days grew longer and warmer. Soon summer had come. Papi grew taller and stronger and spent his days chasing butterflies and playing tag with his cousins. Every evening at twilight ("What's 'twilight'? Papi asked Nika. "That's when the day meets the night, Papi.") the Man Samuel would lead them all into the Great Barn. Papi curled up beside Nika on their bed of straw and dreamed.

It was a good and happy life for a donkey.
The Man Samuel was very kind and gentle.
Papi liked him. Even when the halter was
put on him, Papi was not afraid. He
learned to pull a small cart and
proudly hauled wood to the
house on the hill.

"What an adorable donkey!" The Man
Samuel's wife would say.

"Yes, he is a very good donkey; he will soon be
as fine as his mother Nika." The Man Samuel
would reply.

Papi nearly burst with delight when he told his mother. Nika's eyes glowed soft and warm as she listened to Papi.

"You know Papi, I have not told you this before, but I believe you are old enough now. Your Grandfather was one of the Honored Few."

Papi swallowed. "The Honored Few?" he whispered in awe.

"Yes dear. He travelled many many miles across the desert with the Magi as they searched for the Baby King.

"Oh Mother! Tell me about it, please, please?" And he begged so hard that at last Nika agreed to tell him the whole story that very night.

The rest of that day Papi could hardly wait to hear of his Grandfather's great adventure. He didn't even finish his carrot at dinnertime.

"Now mother? Will you tell me now?"

Nika laughed. "Alright, come lie down and I will tell you of your special heritage."

Papi curled up on his bed of hay.

"What's 'heritage' mother?"

"It means something that is passed down from generation to generation."

"What's 'generation'?" asked Papi.

"Well," said Nika, "Grandfather was part of his generation, I am part of my generation and you are part of your generation, you see?"

"Oh!" said Papi.

"Hush now and listen."

And this is the story that Nika told.

"Long long ago your Grandfather lived with the Man Melkizadek, a very wise and powerful man in the East."

"Was he a king, mother?" asked Papi.

"He was one of the great teachers called 'Magi'. The Man Melkizadek was kind and thoughtful. He read many books and studied them earnestly."

"What does 'earnestly' mean, mother?"

"Well, it means he tried very hard to understand all the things he read."

"Oh!" said Papi.

One day the Man Melkizadek read about a Baby King, a Star, and a prophecy. He became very excited and rushed off to share the news with his colleagues."

"What is 'colleagues' mother?"

"Really, Papi, I shall never get this story told if you keep interrupting! It means 'friends'."

"Oh!" said Papi.

"Yes, and Grandfather says there was a commotion that lasted for many weeks. Visitors from all over came to study with the Man Melkizadek and together they discovered that a Star would appear when the Baby King was born."

"What was his name, mother?"

"Whose name, Papi?"

"Grandfather's".

"Oh!" exclaimed Nika, embarrassed. "His name was Elijah."

"Elijah!" whispered Papi.

"Yes dear." said Nika.

"Several of the wisest Magi decided to devote their time to researching-"

"What's 'researching' mother?"

"'Researching' is like studying, Papi. They researched all the information they could about the Star.

"Months went by. One wondrously warm night, Elijah and the Man Melkizadek went riding as usual, and after a mile or two, Elijah says that the Man Melkizadek jumped off, shouting and singing and dancing around. He threw his arms around Elijah's neck and whispered "Look!"

"Look at what?" shouted Papi.

"Hush Papi! Settle down!"

Elijah looked and there in the clear night sky was a beautiful star, bright and shining, so bright it looked like the sun!"

"The Great Star!" Papi yelled, jumping up in excitement.

"Yes Papi, please, not so loud."

"In no time at all, the Man Melkizadek packed up a vast caravan-"

"What's 'vast', mother?" asked Papi.

"Vast is 'huge'. Remember what I said about interruptions, Papi."

"Oh!" whispered Papi, lying down again.

17

"A huge caravan of camels, horses, donkeys-"

"Grandfather?"

"Yes Papi. Donkeys and servants and plenty of food. The Magi also filled boxes and bags of gifts for the Baby King."

"Lots of presents, mother?"

"Yes Papi, because the Baby King was God's own Son. Early the next morning, they set out on the long journey. They followed the Great Star, which glowed day and night. Grandfather says it took many months of journeying to reach Jerusalem."

"Our Jerusalem?" asked Papi.

"Yes dear, our Jerusalem."

"The Man Melkizadek and his friends went to visit King Herod and ask where the Baby King was, because the Star had stopped right above Jerusalem. Imagine their surprise, Papi, to find that King Herod did not know anything about the Baby King! Instead, King Herod called in his scribes.

"What's 'scribes', mother?

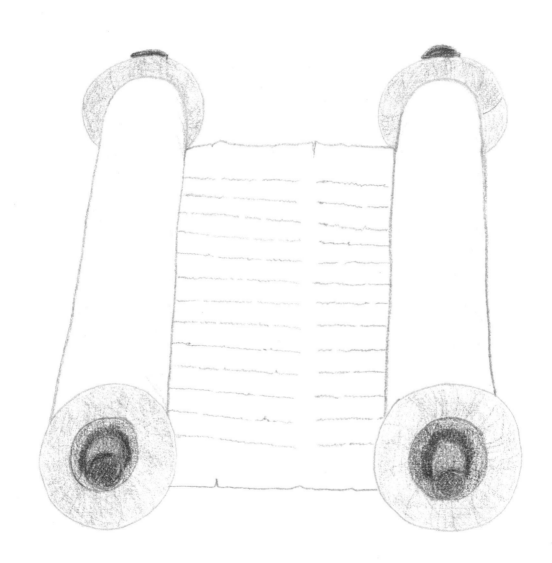

"Scribes are men who write things on scrolls." replied Nika.

"Oh." said Papi. He wanted to ask what a scroll was, but he decided not to.

"King Herod asked the scribes about the legend of the Baby King. They talked with the local priests. They discovered that the Baby King would be born in the town of Bethlehem. Then King Herod told the Magi to go and find the Baby King so he could worship him too."

"Did all the people in Jerusalem go too? Did they find the Baby King? asked Papi.

"No, Papi, not very many people went. And later, as we shall see, the Magi found out that King Herod was lying. He wanted to spy on the Baby King.

"Oh no! What happened, mother, what happened?"

"Then Elijah and his Man Melkizadek and the other Wise men and the other donkeys and the camels all loaded with the gifts for the Baby King moved down the street to the little house where they saw the Messiah himself, a little baby in his mother's arms. They each presented their wonderful gifts.

Papi sighed. "How wonderful to see the Baby King!"

"Yes dear. That is why all the donkeys that were part of that journey are called the Honored Few. You are part of the story now, Papi. I hope you know how important that is."

"I do mother, I do!" exclaimed Papi. "What happened to the Baby King and to Grandfather Elijah?

"After they gave the Baby King the gifts, the Wise men with their caravan turned around and began their long journey back home. Grandfather Elijah stayed behind to help the family of the Baby King."

"Really mother? Really truly?"

"Yes Papi. Then God told the Baby King's family to leave quickly to get away from King Herod. In the middle of the night they packed and went on their way. All those gifts helped them while they lived so far from home."

Nika lay down beside Papi. Maybe one day you will meet another donkey who is so blessed."

"What do you mean, mother?"

"Well, you see, there is another prophecy about the Baby King, only of course, now he is the Grown up Messiah Himself."

25

"According to one of the scrolls that Grandfather Elijah heard his Man Melkizadek reading, one day the Messiah will "…ride through the gates of Jerusalem on a colt, one never before ridden".

Papi was so excited, he wished he could talk all night about the adventures of Grandfather Elijah and the Baby King, but his eyes were so heavy! He decided to close them for just a minute. Soon Papi was fast asleep.

After the story, Papi became more and more eager to do his work. He said to himself, "My very own Grandfather was one of the Honored Few. I must do my best to make mother proud of me."

Every night Papi would curl up on the nice warm hay and think of the prophecy, and how wonderful it would be to see the Lord King ride into Jerusalem.

Papi was soon as big and strong as his mother, Nika. All the Man Samuel's children loved him and played with him every day.

One evening, all the animals in the Great Barn were very excited, even the sheep were whispering among themselves. Papi was curious. "What is it mama? He asked.

"A special occasion, Papi. It is called the Passover Celebration, and a few of us will be chosen to go with our Man Samuel to the village tomorrow!" whispered Nika.

Papi jumped up and down. "Really mother?" Nika laughed and said, "Hush Papi, go to sleep!"

Imagine Papi's surprise the next morning when all the Man Samuel's children came to the barn and both he and Nika were led out into the bright sunshine. The Man Samuel rode on Nika and Papi came walking right beside her. He was going to town!

Papi was so excited he kept turning around until the Man Samuel laughed and laughed. Nika whispered, "Calm down Papi, before you trip over your own feet!" Papi tried very hard to be calm, but there were people and donkeys and camels and sheep and houses; so much to see!

At last they were inside the village. Nika and Papi stood in the shade, munching on some sweet grass. "Ah, we can rest for awhile!" sighed Nika. She closed her eyes for a nap. But Papi did not want to sleep, oh no! He wanted to see every little thing and even let some nearby children pet his nose.

So many wonderful smells and colors and sounds! How exciting the village was! He decided he wanted to stay for a long time and was about to tell his mother when two strangers walked up to him.

Papi stepped backward right into Nika, who woke suddenly. She called loudly for the Man Samuel.

"What are you doing?" asked the Man Samuel as he came around the corner. The stranger nearest to Papi cleared his throat and said "The Lord needs them, sir".

Papi looked from the stranger to the Man Samuel. For a moment all was silent.

"What are they doing, mother?" asked Papi.

"Don't be afraid." Said Nika, trembling.

Then the Man Samuel handed the rope to the stranger! Papi was led through the crowded street and up a hill. He wanted to ask so many questions, but Nika did not answer except to say "Hush, Papi." At the top of the hill, they stopped. A crowd was there, but all were silent, and Papi was frightened. "What is happening mother?" he cried.

A Man beside him patted him gently. His voice was gentle and low. "Don't be afraid little one, I will not harm you."

"Papi, do what he says… I have a strange feeling about this…" said Nika softly.

Dozens of feet surrounded them; Papi didn't know where to turn. Suddenly, he couldn't see Nika. "Mother? Where are you?" he shouted.

"I am right behind you dear."

The Man at his side bent down and touched Papi's nose very softly. "Thank you, little one!" he said. All of a sudden, the Man was on his back! What an odd, feeling! Not at all like hauling wood! But it wasn't scary. The Man began to whisper so Papi listened very carefully.

As they walked along the dusty trail, more and more people were joining in the march. Papi kept his head up and listened to the Man's voice. Soon, someone started singing, and then more people joined in, and then more. Laughing and dancing they filled the path all around Papi, Nika and the Stranger.

By the time the trail turned downward toward the valley, there were so many people it was hard to even put one hoof in front of the other! Papi turned his head and looked at Nika. He saw great tears in her eyes. "Mama? What is it? He's not hurting me at all, Mama."

Nika moved closer beside him. "I am so very proud of you my son!"

Papi felt so happy. He did not know why everyone was so excited; he just knew that the Man on his back was kind and that he was going to do his best to carry Him wherever He led.

Down into the valley they went, and as they came around the bend, the sunlight flashed ahead and outlined the Great Golden Gate of Jerusalem. It was right there in front of them! Now the people were laying down their coats in front of Papi's feet. Huge palm branches were being waved on both sides of the road. The songs hushed and someone shouted "Blessed is He who comes in the Name of the Lord!"

The Man on his back urged him toward The Golden Gate. Papi walked, careful not to trip on the robes beneath him. The Man asked him to stop right next to the Gate. Proudly Papi stepped forward. All of a sudden, he knew. He Knew! And Papi felt he would burst with happiness!

He began to shout "Look! Look! Mother, it is the Great King's Son! I am the Honored One! Oh, look! I am the Honored One!'

No one in the excited crown noticed tears of joy falling from Nika and Papi's eyes as they continued into the city of Jerusalem. The little donkey walked as proudly and gratefully as he could, for he was carrying the King, the Greatest King, upon his back.

About the Author

Sherri is a free-lance writer, poet and artist who has an insatiable love of ancient history and inspirational themes. Bringing it all together in the Little Donkey Adventures is a long-time dream come true for her. Sherri lives in the Pacific Northwest with her husband and a very mischievous puppy. Her next pet will be a donkey.